This book belongs to

....

Peppa Pig

LADYBIRD BOOKS

UK | USA | Canada | Ireland | Australia | India | New Zealand | South Africa

Ladybird Books is part of the Penguin Random House group of companies
whose addresses can be found at global.penguinrandomhouse.com.

www.penguin.co.uk   www.puffin.co.uk   www.ladybird.co.uk

Penguin
Random House
UK

First published 2022
001

Licensed by

Hasbro   eOne

Printed in China

The authorized representative in the EEA is Penguin Random House Ireland,
Morrison Chambers, 32 Nassau Street, Dublin D02 YH68

A CIP catalogue record for this book is available from the British Library

ISBN: 978-0-241-54340-5

All correspondence to:
Ladybird Books, Penguin Random House Children's
One Embassy Gardens, 8 Viaduct Gardens, London SW11 7BW

FSC
www.fsc.org
MIX
Paper from
responsible sources
FSC® C018179

Peppa Loves E♥eryone

Peppa and her friends had just arrived at playgroup.
"Morning, children," said Madame Gazelle. "Today we
are going to think about what makes us all special."
"Ooooh!" cried the children.

Ooooh!

"Together we are **one** lovely playgroup class," said Madame Gazelle, "but each of us is very **different**."

"I have wavy horns on my head," said Madame Gazelle, picking up her guitar. "And I like to sing."
"Your horns are *very* beautiful, Madame Gazelle," said Peppa.

"Thank you, Peppa," said Madame Gazelle. "That's very kind."
"I love singing with you," said Pedro Pony.
"Thank you, Pedro," said Madame Gazelle. "I love singing
with you, too."

Madame Gazelle asked the children to draw pictures of what made *them* special.
"I'm drawing myself tall," said Gerald Giraffe, "and with a basketball. I love playing basketball!"

"I love basketball, too," said Mandy Mouse.
"I'm going to draw myself whizzing around
with the ball. And lots of cheese! I *love* cheese!"

Zoe Zebra drew lots of black-and-white stripes.
"Me and my family have stripes," she said.
"I love my stripes. *And* I love
playing the recorder."

"I love carrots!"
said Rebecca Rabbit,
drawing a giant
orange carrot.

Molly Mole drew herself wearing her favourite
glasses and digging for buried treasure.

And George drew a
big green . . . "Dine-saw.
Grr!" roared George.

Grr!

Peggi and Pandora Panda drew themselves together . . .
but their pictures looked different.
"Being twins makes us special," said Pandora.
"We look the same, and like *some* of the same things," said Peggi.
"Like solving mysteries," added Pandora.
"But we like different things, too," said Peggi.

"Excellent," said Madame Gazelle. "We are all *unique*. That means that, even if we look similar, we are not exactly the same."

"What are you drawing,
Edmond?" asked
Madame Gazelle.
"All the planets in the
solar system!" said
Edmond Elephant proudly.
"I know lots about space.
That makes me special."
Edmond is a bit of a
clever clogs.

"Wonderful," said Madame Gazelle. She looked around.
"What amazing pictures, children. They're all different
and very special indeed."

Peppa put up her hand. "Madame Gazelle," she said, "I'm not a twin, but I do like basketball and space a little bit . . ." "Don't worry, Peppa," said Madame Gazelle. "You don't need to draw those things."

"But I don't know what else to draw," said Peppa.
"You could try doing your drawing at home," said Madame Gazelle. "I'm sure you will think of something there."
"Yes!" said Peppa. "I'll try!"

It was time to go home, and the children's parents had come to pick them up.

"Next time," said Madame Gazelle, "we are going to have a party to celebrate how different we all are."

"Hooray!" cheered the children.
"I'd like you all to bring some of
your favourite things with you to
playgroup," added Madame Gazelle.
"Hooray!" everyone cheered again.

Hooray!

At home, Peppa talked to Mummy and Daddy Pig
about her drawing and the party. "I don't know
what to draw or bring in," she said, sighing.
"There are lots of things that make you special, Peppa,"
said Mummy Pig.

"Yes," agreed Daddy Pig, "and you have lots of favourite things."
"Why don't we try doing some to see if that helps you decide?" said Mummy Pig.
"That's a great idea!" said Peppa.

Peppa had lots of fun trying some of her favourite things.

"I love Teddy," said Peppa,

"... and playing in my den with my magical unicorn."

"I also love going to the playground," said Peppa,

"...and jumping
in muddy puddles."

But Peppa still couldn't
decide what to draw or
bring to the party!

"I love so many things," said Peppa. "But they are much better when I do them with my friends. Everything is better with my friends . . . That's it!" she cried. "I'm going to need a big piece of paper, please, Daddy."

"Of course, Peppa," said Daddy Pig.
"Coming right up!"

Peppa sat down at
the kitchen table and
got to work . . .

On the day of the playgroup party, the children brought in lots of things to share with everyone.

Mandy had her favourite cheese . . .

Gerald had his basketball . . .

George and Richard Rabbit had their dinosaurs . . .

Grrr!

Not everyone loved Mandy's cheese, or playing basketball, or dinosaurs, but they all had lots of fun sharing and trying different things.

When it was Peppa's turn, she showed Madame Gazelle the picture she'd drawn at home.
"I love doing everything with my friends," said Peppa, "so I drew all my friends. They make me feel special."

"How wonderful, Peppa!" said Madame Gazelle.
"And I know something all my friends love to do . . ."
said Peppa, heading outside.

"...Jump in muddy puddles!" cheered Peppa.
The playgroup friends couldn't wait to play in the mud
with Peppa, and they all did it in their own special way.

Splish!

Splash!

They splashed, whizzed around, spun, danced and played their very own favourite muddy-puddle games . . .

Hee! Hee!

Hee! Hee!

Splash!

"What makes me special," said Peppa, "is all my friends!"

"I think what makes you special, Peppa," said Madame Gazelle,
"is that you know how to make all your friends smile."
"Hooray!" cheered Peppa's friends.

Peppa loves everyone.
And everyone loves Peppa!